Teacher

Jeff Barger

Rourke™

ROURKE'S
SCHOOL to HOME
CONNECTIONS

BEFORE AND DURING READING ACTIVITIES

Before Reading: *Building Background Knowledge and Vocabulary*

Building background knowledge can help children process new information and build upon what they already know. Before reading a book, it is important to tap into what children already know about the topic. This will help them develop their vocabulary and increase their reading comprehension.

Questions and Activities to Build Background Knowledge:

1. Look at the front cover of the book and read the title. What do you think this book will be about?
2. What do you already know about this topic?
3. Take a book walk and skim the pages. Look at the table of contents, photographs, captions, and bold words. Did these text features give you any information or predictions about what you will read in this book?

Vocabulary: *Vocabulary Is Key to Reading Comprehension*

Use the following directions to prompt a conversation about each word.

- Read the vocabulary words.
- What comes to mind when you see each word?
- What do you think each word means?

Vocabulary Words:
- *college*
- *lesson*
- *model*
- *principals*

During Reading: *Reading for Meaning and Understanding*

To achieve deep comprehension of a book, children are encouraged to use close reading strategies. During reading, it is important to have children stop and make connections. These connections result in deeper analysis and understanding of a book.

Close Reading a Text

During reading, have children stop and talk about the following:

- Any confusing parts
- Any unknown words
- Text to text, text to self, text to world connections
- The main idea in each chapter or heading

Encourage children to use context clues to determine the meaning of any unknown words. These strategies will help children learn to analyze the text more thoroughly as they read.

When you are finished reading this book, turn to the next-to-last page for an **After Reading Activity**.

Table of Contents

Community Helpers

Community helpers are all around us. They make our lives better.

Teachers work at schools.

These helpers lead students.

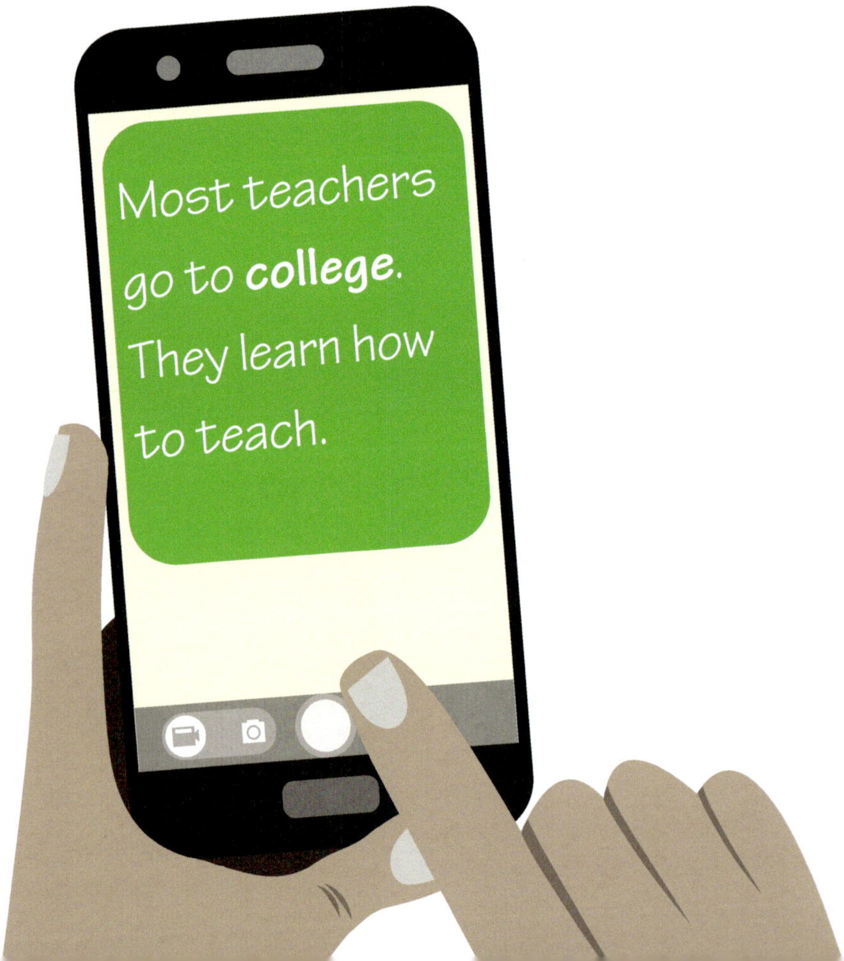

In Class

The day starts. The teacher greets students as they come in.

The bell rings.

The teacher is ready to begin.

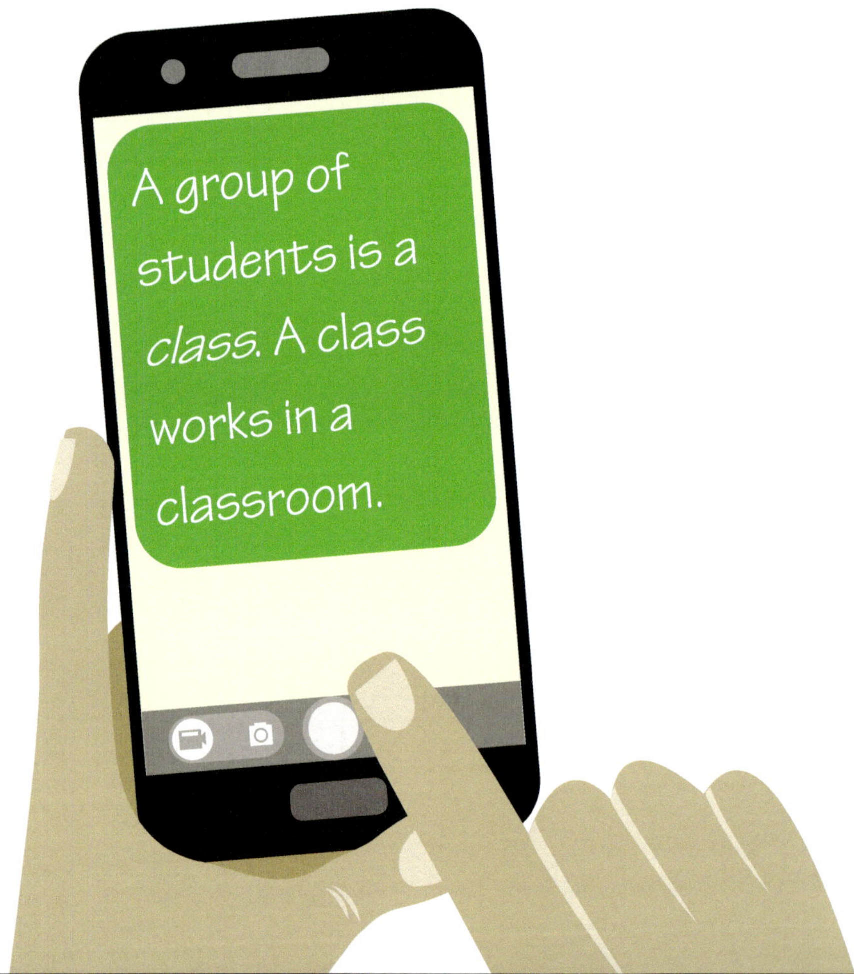

live out people
who work
6. bike
7. dime
8. hide
9. ice
10. kite
get
use

This **lesson** is about adding.

An example is given.

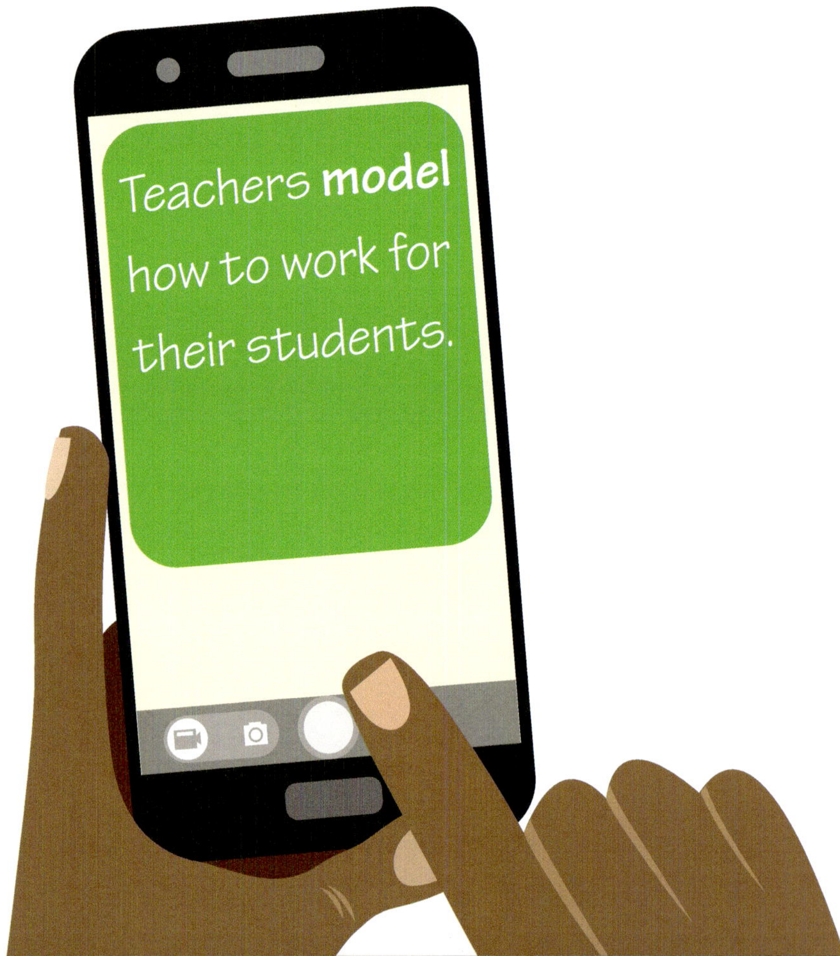

1+1=2
2+2=

The class adds. They write.

The teacher listens as they talk.

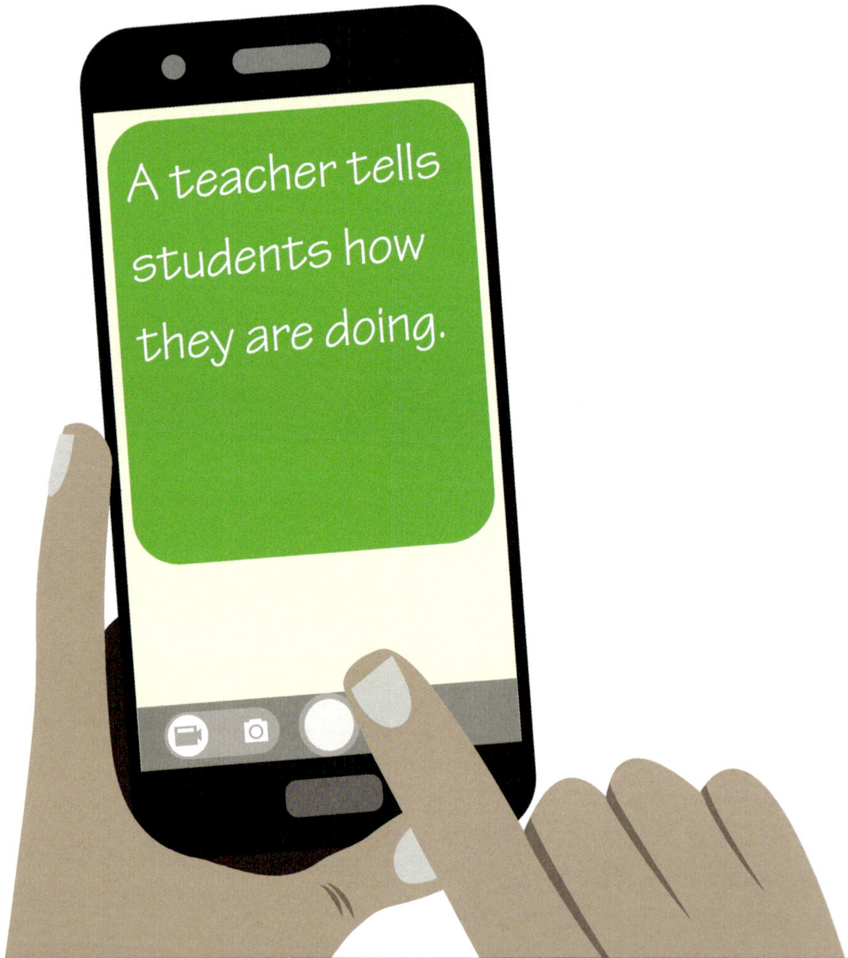

After School

It is the end of the day.

Teachers walk students to the bus.

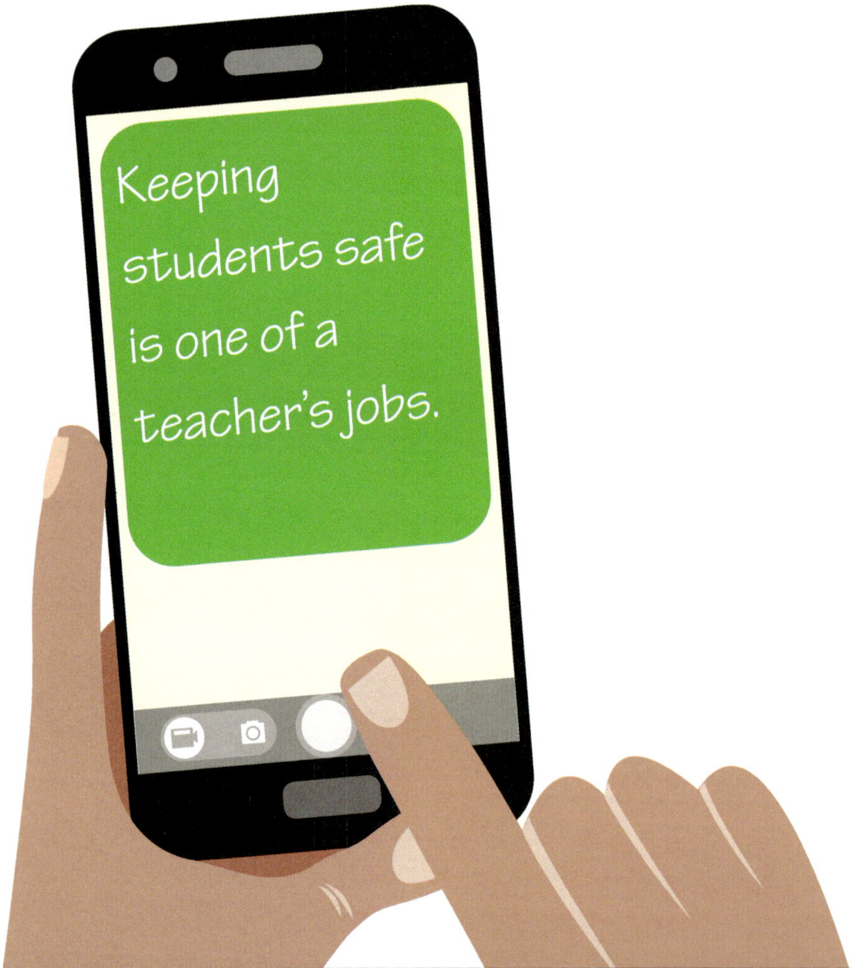

Teachers meet after school.

They talk about helping students.

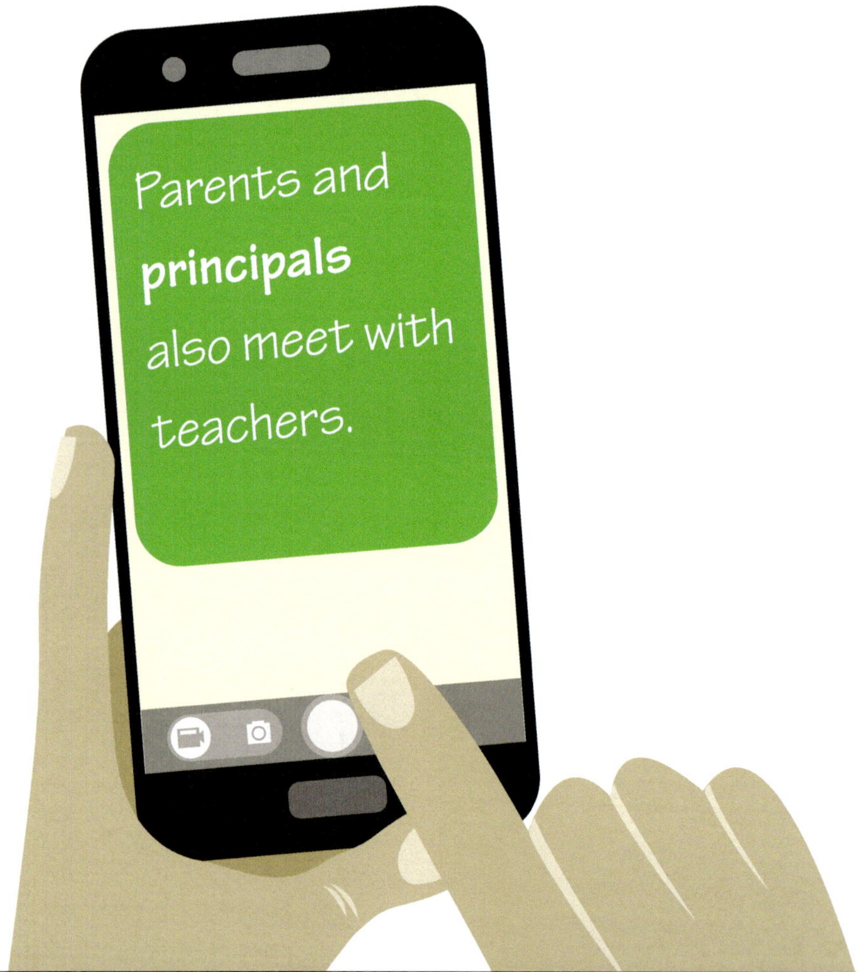

Teachers help kids learn and grow. They are important to a community.

Activity

Interview with Your Teacher

An interview is when you ask someone questions. What would you like to ask your teacher?

Supplies

- paper
- pencil

Directions

1. Think about what questions you would like to ask. For example, "Why did you become a teacher?" could be a question.
2. Write three questions. Leave space below each question.
3. Ask your teacher these questions. Write each answer below the question.
4. Share your interview with a partner.

Photo Glossary

college (KAH-lij): A place for students to learn and study after they have finished high school.

lesson (LES-uhn): What students are taught during one time period at school.

model (MAH-duhl): To show how to do something.

principals (PRIN-suh-puhls): People who are in charge of schools.

Index

After Reading Activity

Pretend you are teaching someone how to make a sandwich. On a piece of paper, write the steps you would teach.

About the Author

Jeff Barger is an author, blogger, and literacy specialist. He lives in North Carolina. Jeff has been a teacher for 30 years. He has sharpened thousands of pencils.

www.rourkebooks.com

Edited by: Kim Thompson
Cover and interior design by: Kathy Walsh

Photo Credits: Cover, title page, p.7, 20, 22: ©PeopleImages; p.5: ©Rawpixel.com; p.9: ©BraunS; p.11: ©monkeybusinessimages; p.13, 17, 22: ©Wavebreakmedia; p.15: ©Ridofranz; p.19, 22: ©Lokibaho

Library of Congress PCN Data

Teacher / Jeff Barger
(Community Helpers)
ISBN 978-1-73161-422-3 (hard cover)(alk. paper)
ISBN 978-1-73161-217-5 (soft cover)
ISBN 978-1-73161-527-5 (e-Book)
ISBN 978-1-73161-632-6 (ePub)
Library of Congress Control Number: 2019932039

Rourke Educational Media
Printed in the United States of America
01-2972211937